Grandma Is Prob

Not A Witch.

A.S. Cureton

A. S. Cureton

Grandma Is Probably Not a Witch

Pegasus

PEGASUS PAPERBACK

A CIP catalogue record for this title is
available from the British Library

ISBN- 978 1 91090 338 4

Pegasus is an imprint of
Pegasus Elliot MacKenzie Publishers Ltd.
www.pegasuspublishers.com

First Published in 2020

Pegasus
Sheraton House Castle Park
Cambridge CB3 0AX England

Printed & Bound in Great Britain

For Larzy and Ripley.

This is me and my Grandma.

She's not a witch, at least I definitely think she's probably not one.

Although I suppose, she does look a little bit like a witch.

And her house looks slightly witchy…

13

And for some reason, is bigger inside than out…

Her garden is a bit like the sort of garden you
would expect a witch to have, but that doesn’t prove anything.

She does have a black cat...

...That can talk.

But my friend's Grandma has a parrot that can also talk, and no-one calls her a witch.

Grandma cooks me very strange food.

Which she serves out of a cauldron.

COOKING WITH CHILDREN
ar tom

And the food quite often has unwanted side-effects.

It is true that she turned that man into a frog.

But Grandma says he deserved it.

Grandma's friends are not the sort of people you'd expect a Grandma to have but just because they're weird, doesn't mean that she's a witch, does it?

BIG Book of SPELLS
BEHEMOTH

I think lots of grandmas probably have magic
mirrors that lie to them about how pretty they are,
so I shouldn't read anything into that.

Grandma sometimes picks me up from school…

WXYZ
SHUT UP
AND
LEARN
MEG
JAMIE
AVA
Problem 1:
Mrs Witch's
oven CAN FIT
HILDREN
RE ARE
REN HOW
OES

...On her broomstick.

She doesn't seem to get on very well with her neighbours.

But Grandma says that's their problem.

13

Would a Grandma who happened to be a witch
take me to such brilliant parties?!

Anyway, Grandma says that everyone better stop calling her a witch.

Unless they want to end up tiny, slimy and green and living in a jar…